The Cave of Snores

DENNIS HASELEY

The Cave of Snores

illustrated by Eric Beddows

Fitzhenry & Whiteside
Toronto, Ottawa, Halifax
Winnipeg, Edmonton
Vancouver

The Cave of Snores
Text copyright © 1987 by Dennis Haseley
Illustrations copyright © 1987 by Eric Beddows
All rights reserved
No part of this publication may be
reproduced in any form, or by any means,
without permission in writing
from the publisher.
Fitzhenry & Whiteside Limited
195 Allstate Parkway
Markham, Ontario L3R 4T8
ISBN 0-88902-933-4

Canadian Cataloguing in Publication Data
Haseley, Dennis
    The cave of snores

ISBN 0-88902-933-4
I. Beddows, Eric, 1951–   . II. Title.
PZ7.H2688Ca 1987   j813'.54   C86-094698-3

To my father, who snores,
and my mother, who listens

The Cave of Snores

One night, as we were falling asleep, my father started to tell me about the cave of snores. "I found it once," he said. "It was a hole like an open mouth." He stretched and yawned. "I was scared," he whispered, "as scared as my own father had been..."

But before he could go on with his story, he dropped off to sleep and began to snore. His snores rose like trumpet notes into the night. At their campfire, the shepherds cursed and shouted; and someone threw a boot that landed near my head.

Gomal, with his half-closed eyes, said, "Those snores make the sheep crabby; and they keep me awake, so I am crabby too!"

Ketzof stood and spoke in his voice like a goat's: "Those snores tell the wolves where we a-a-aare…"

Josef shivered in his long coat and said, "The robber Kabul with one finger missing comes and carries off our sheep. Why? Because those snores hide the sound of his fat belly dragging over the rocks!"

I wanted to run up to their fire and tell them what my father said about his snores.

"If my father's snores find you crabby, they will leave you crabby," I wanted to say. "But if your dreams are sweet, his snores will make them sweeter."

Gomal would listen and nod.

"My father's snores jump out like big dogs when the wolves are near," I wanted to say, "and chase the wolves away."

Ketzof would listen and nod.

I wanted to say, "When fat Kabul comes with his men to carry off our sheep, my father's snores roll out like big iron balls. And the bandits run, for they have seen such iron balls chained to the legs of prisoners!"

Josef would listen solemnly and nod.

Then all three would say, "Move your tent close to us—close, close."

And I would nod.

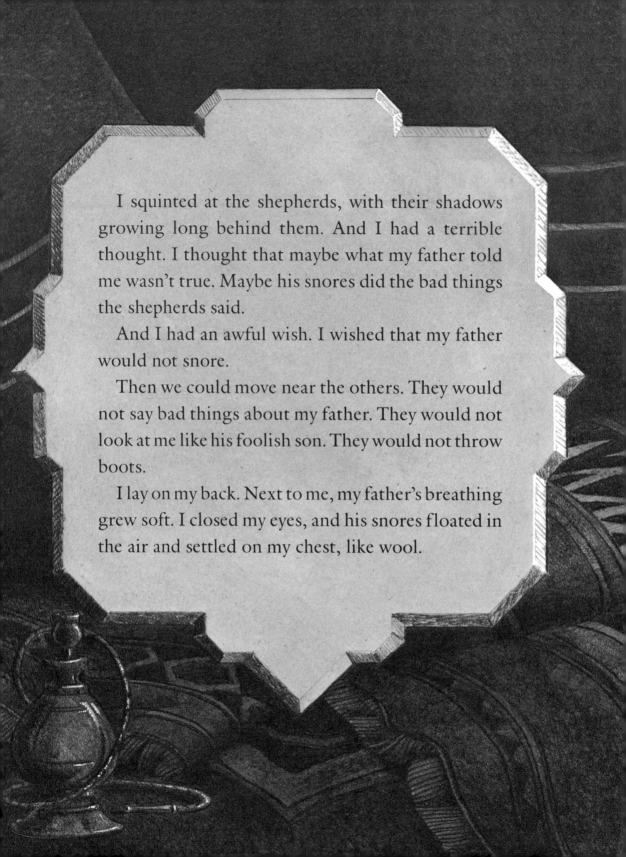

I squinted at the shepherds, with their shadows growing long behind them. And I had a terrible thought. I thought that maybe what my father told me wasn't true. Maybe his snores did the bad things the shepherds said.

And I had an awful wish. I wished that my father would not snore.

Then we could move near the others. They would not say bad things about my father. They would not look at me like his foolish son. They would not throw boots.

I lay on my back. Next to me, my father's breathing grew soft. I closed my eyes, and his snores floated in the air and settled on my chest, like wool.

I wanted to say, "When fat Kabul comes with his men to carry off our sheep, my father's snores roll out like big iron balls. And the bandits run, for they have seen such iron balls chained to the legs of prisoners!"

Josef would listen solemnly and nod.

Then all three would say, "Move your tent close to us—close, close."

And I would nod.

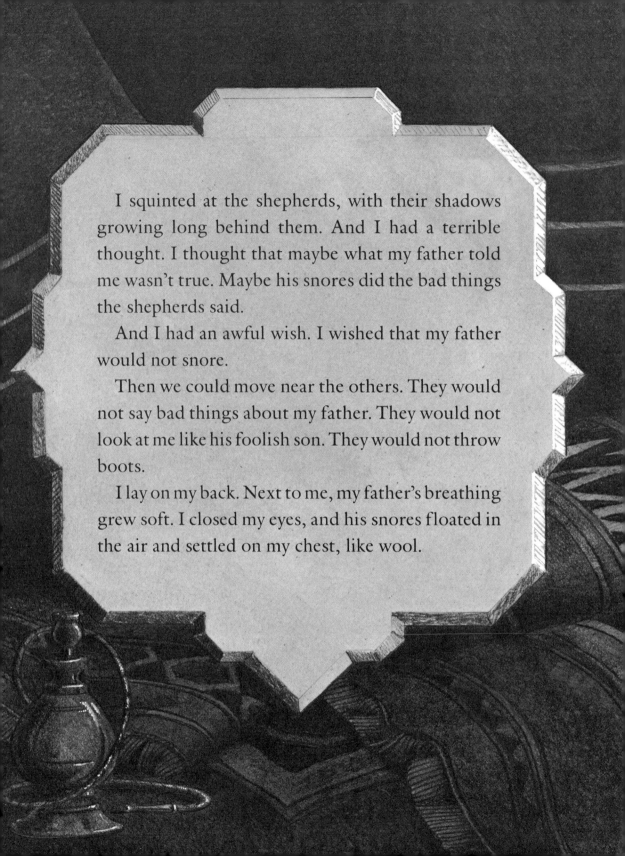

I squinted at the shepherds, with their shadows growing long behind them. And I had a terrible thought. I thought that maybe what my father told me wasn't true. Maybe his snores did the bad things the shepherds said.

And I had an awful wish. I wished that my father would not snore.

Then we could move near the others. They would not say bad things about my father. They would not look at me like his foolish son. They would not throw boots.

I lay on my back. Next to me, my father's breathing grew soft. I closed my eyes, and his snores floated in the air and settled on my chest, like wool.

It was still dark when I woke. My father was snoring loudly. I heard footsteps coming toward us—and the shepherds entered. With them was a fat man. I could not see his face, for he was wearing the hat of a wizard.

"Have you come to visit us?" I asked, but my voice came out in a high squeak. "I will wake my father."

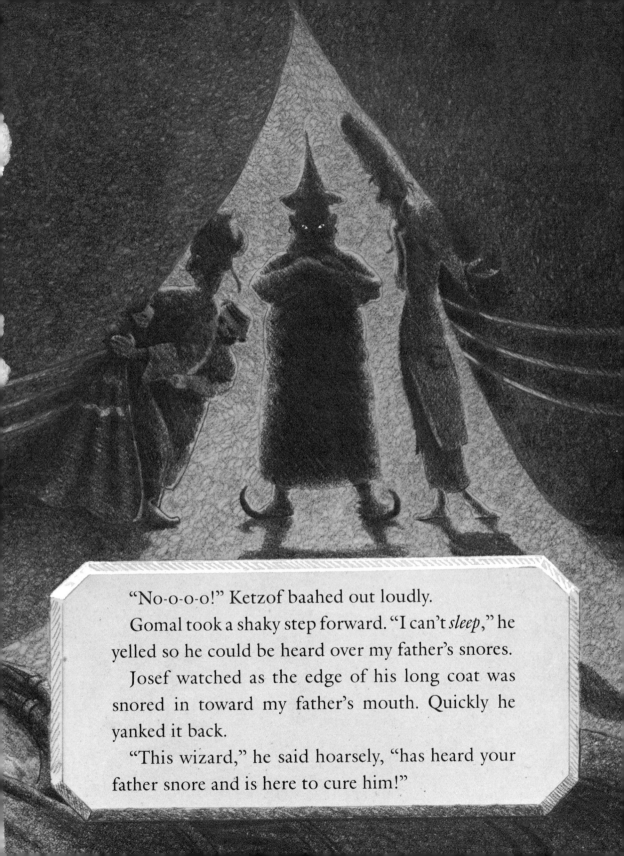

"No-o-o-o!" Ketzof baahed out loudly.

Gomal took a shaky step forward. "I can't *sleep*," he yelled so he could be heard over my father's snores.

Josef watched as the edge of his long coat was snored in toward my father's mouth. Quickly he yanked it back.

"This wizard," he said hoarsely, "has heard your father snore and is here to cure him!"

Suddenly I knew there was danger, and I was going to yell out, I *was*, but that wizard grinned at me and put his hand over my mouth. It smelled of garlic and sheep fat. With his other hand he took powder from his pocket and dropped it into my sleeping father's open mouth.

One big smoky snore drifted out like a cloud.

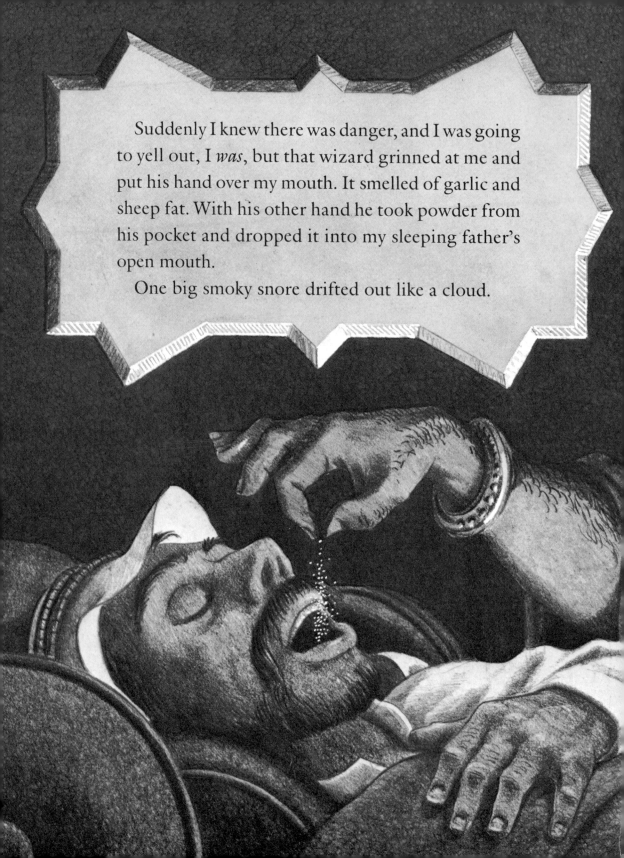

Then there was silence.

The wizard laughed and pushed me roughly away as he and the others left our tent. I tried to wake my father, but he slept on and on. So I crawled under my blanket and lay awake, while the night stretched silent all around me, like stone.

In the morning I told my father what had happened. He listened, smoking his pipe, and his beard looked darker, as it did when he was angry.

"Tell me about the wizard," he said.

"He was big," I answered, "and smelly." I closed my eyes. Again I felt the wizard's smelly hand over my mouth.

"And one of his fingers was missing!" I cried.

"Kabul," said my father. "Now there is danger for us."

Slowly he smoked his pipe, while I looked down at my feet. I felt he was looking into me, seeing my wish.

Night after night now, misfortune struck. Without my father's soft snores, the sheep grew mean and bit our hands, and many fell down cliffs in the night. Without his fierce snores, the wolves came into our flocks.

But the worst was Kabul. With his cowardly men he sneaked up on our sheep, and the spaces in the herd grew rock by rock by rock…

"Kabul," said my father. "Now there is danger for us."

Slowly he smoked his pipe, while I looked down at my feet. I felt he was looking into me, seeing my wish.

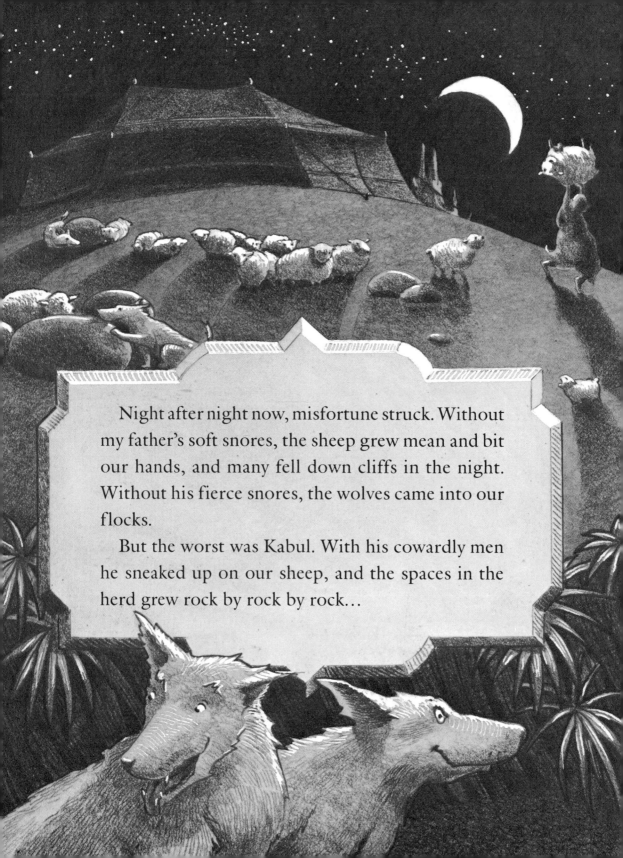

Night after night now, misfortune struck. Without my father's soft snores, the sheep grew mean and bit our hands, and many fell down cliffs in the night. Without his fierce snores, the wolves came into our flocks.

But the worst was Kabul. With his cowardly men he sneaked up on our sheep, and the spaces in the herd grew rock by rock by rock…

The shepherds came again. "I'm sleeping worse now," grumbled Gomal.

Ketzof gave a high laugh. "I really always liked your sno-o-o-ores," he said.

Josef tried to smile. "I will lend you my long coat, given to me by a judge, if only you will play the music of your nose again," he said.

My father looked them up and down and puffed on his pipe. There was nothing to be done, he said. The magic powder worked too well; he thought he would always sleep in silence.

That night I tried to stay awake, keeping watch. I thought I heard a sound over my father's quiet breathing—a sound of distant snores.

I knew what I must do.

I dressed in the cold and stumbled into the dark toward the mountain paths where only the goats go. Walking past rocks huddled like bandits, and past bandits watching as still as rocks, I listened for the cave of snores.

But I heard nothing—no snores, or even wind. There was only my breath, quick in my chest, and the silent yellow eyes of a wolf.

I came to a cliff and bushes growing thick and coarse as a beard. I pushed through to a hollow blacker than the stone around it.

And my heart beat fast. A cave!

I pushed into the cave, brushing cobwebs from my face, and tripped. I leaned back in the dark—and a small tunnel opened in the rough wall behind me!

Putting my ear to its mouth, I listened. Nothing. So I crawled in farther, and the silence closed around me, thick as cloth. I edged in farther, farther than I had ever gone down into the ground.

As I moved, I sensed the roof opening, and I thought I heard a sound in the dark, like the earth's breath. I stood then, and in a small voice I said, "Is someone there who can make my father snore?"

There was no answer.

"Please," I said more boldly, "please make my father snore again."

I went in three more steps, and stopped.

For suddenly I knew there was no cave of snores. There was nothing in this hole or any hole of rock but me. And I felt a cave—very black and deep— opening inside me.

I turned to run away. But it was black, and the walls had turned to empty space, wide as the night. There was only the cold stone beneath my feet. I knelt down and touched it. I knelt there for a long time, so weak I felt, and alone.

I started to cry.

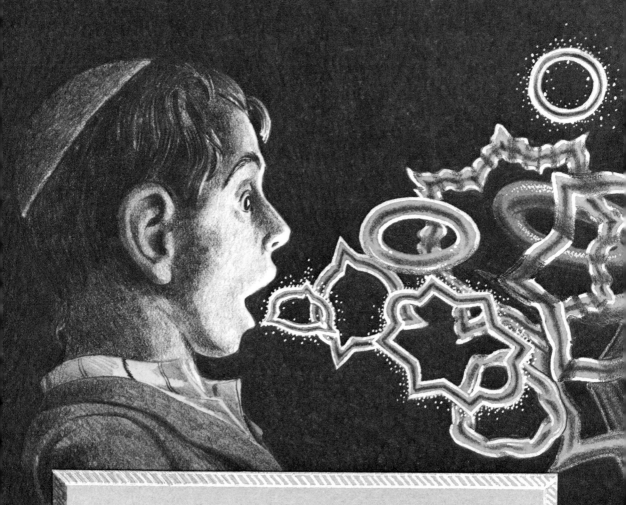

But the crying did not come out like sobs. It came out like snores! Like the fierce snores of my father!

I stood up and felt my breath come out of me, full and deep—my own snores! I made them loud like trees crashing, wild like a red bird flying toward the sun! I made them soft as a horn heard far off in the woods. They echoed and filled that cave!

Then I saw where the cave opened back into the night.

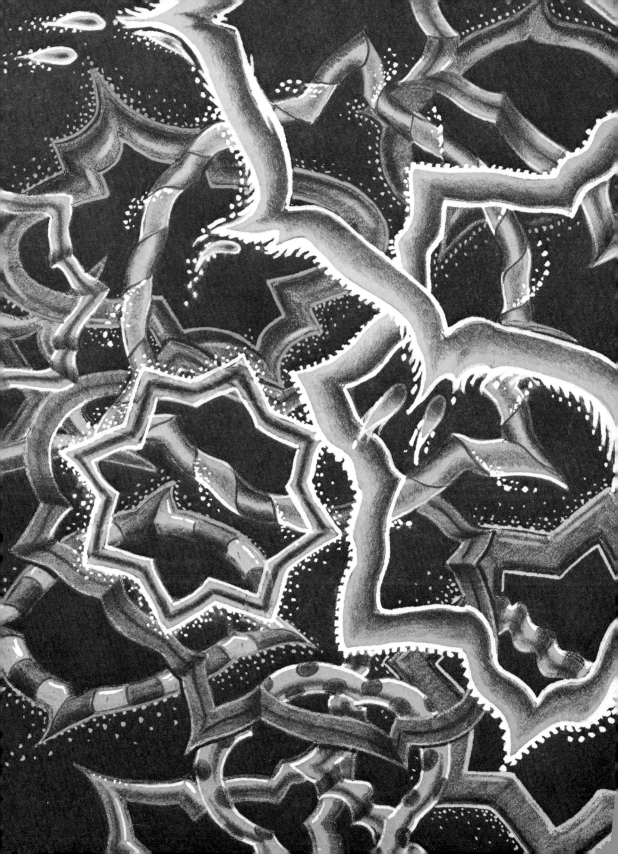

I walked out. When I glanced back for an instant,
that cave looked like my father's open mouth.

I turned and walked on, breathing deep and full,
knowing that my snores were there inside me.

Down the mountain I went. Ahead of me I saw our
camp in danger. The sheep were milling and the
wolves were circling and the moon was going down,
and Kabul with his band of thieves was creeping
closer.

So I crawled into our tent, where my father had not
stirred, and I did what I had to do.

I went to sleep.

Ah! Such a sound came from me as I slept in that tent! It was a sound like great bearded men beating on the ground with clubs. It was a sound like boulders flying off a mountain.

In the middle of the night my father woke and listened. And in the morning he smiled. "Good," he said. "It's about time," and would say no more.

But that night he snored again, and snores flew up from the two of us like a storm.

Again the shepherds came to our tent. "Your snores," said Gomal, "are sweeter than a lullaby." My father looked at me and nodded.

"Your snores," said Ketzof, "jump out like lions when the wolves are near and chase the wolves away." My father and I listened, and solemnly we nodded.

"Your snores," said Josef, hugging his long coat to him, "thunder like hoofbeats and blast like trumpet charges! And Kabul runs, for he thinks it is the wild horses and bugles of the town guard chasing him!"

My father and I listened solemnly and, slowly and solemnly, we nodded.

"Move close to us, close close," they all said at once, "for your wonderful snoring is like two kinds of music."

My father looked them up and down and smiled. And I smiled. Then we smiled at each other.

"Good," said my father. "It's about time."

And I did not mind that every night after that,
I saw Josef and Ketzof and Gomal stuff their ears
with wool.